As the Crow Flies

A FIRST BOOK OF MAPS

by Gail Hartman
illustrated by Harvey Stevenson

Bradbury Press   New York

Collier Macmillan Canada • Toronto
Maxwell Macmillan International Publishing Group
New York • Oxford • Singapore • Sydney

Bradbury Press
Macmillan Publishing Company
866 Third Avenue
New York, NY 10022

Collier Macmillan Canada, Inc.
1200 Eglinton Avenue East
Suite 200
Don Mills, Ontario M3C 3N1

First American edition
Printed in Hong Kong by South China Printing Company (1988) Ltd.
1 2 3 4 5 6 7 8 9 10

The text of this book is set in Souvenir Light.
The illustrations are rendered in pen and ink and watercolor.
Typography by Julie Quan and Christy Hale.

Library of Congress Cataloging-in-Publication Data
Hartman, Gail.
As the crow flies: a first book of maps   / by Gail Hartman;
illustrated by Harvey Stevenson — 1st American ed.
p.   cm.
Summary: A look at different geographical areas from the
perspectives of an eagle, rabbit, crow, horse, and gull.
ISBN 0-02-743005-7
[1. Animals — Fiction. 2. Geography — Fiction.] I. Stevenson, Harvey,
ill. II. Title.
PZ7.H26733As 1990 [E] — dc20 90-33982 CIP AC

For my mom
— G.H.

For Rose
— H.S.

AS THE EAGLE SOARS

From the mountains, a stream flows

through a meadow

where a tall tree
stands.

6

mountains

stream

tree

meadow

THE EAGLE'S MAP

7

A path winds around a farmhouse,

past a shed,

to a garden where the sweet greens grow.

garden

shed

farmhouse

my house

THE RABBIT'S MAP

11

AS THE CROW FLIES

A road runs through fields,

past the factory,

to city streets lined with houses.

factory

city

fields

THE CROW'S MAP

*AS THE
HORSE
TROTS*

In the city, past the hot dog stand

and skyscrapers,

there is a park where music and the
sounds of children playing fill the air.

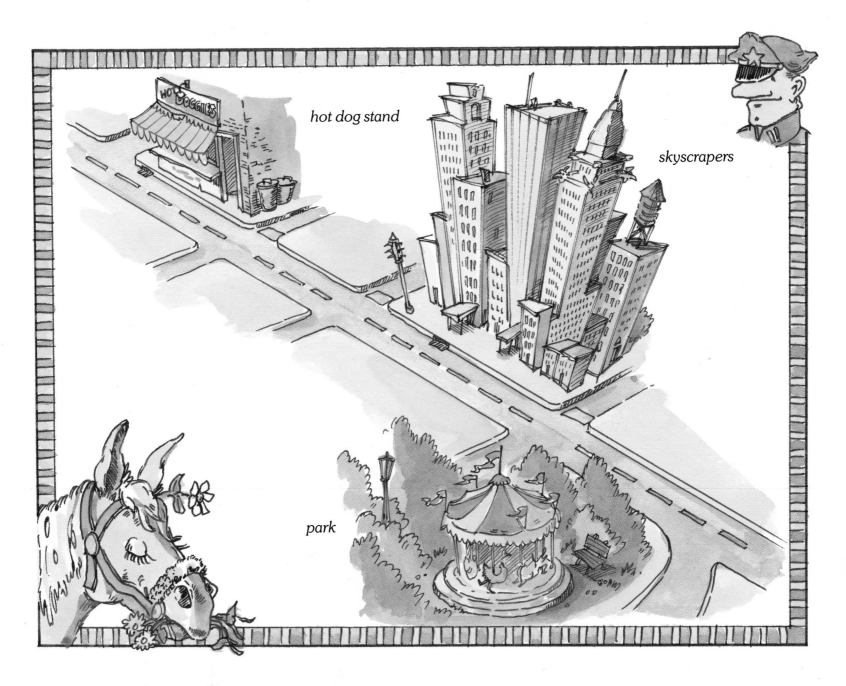

hot dog stand

skyscrapers

park

THE HORSE'S MAP

19

AS THE GULL GLIDES

Beyond the fishing boats in the harbor,

near the red brick lighthouse,

the ocean laps the shores of an island.

lighthouse

ocean

harbor

island

THE GULL'S MAP

When the moon shines, it shines on
the shores of the island in the ocean.

It shines on the park

and the houses in the city.

It shines on the garden near
the farmhouse in the country

27

28

and on the tree in the meadow,

near mountains that touch the sky.

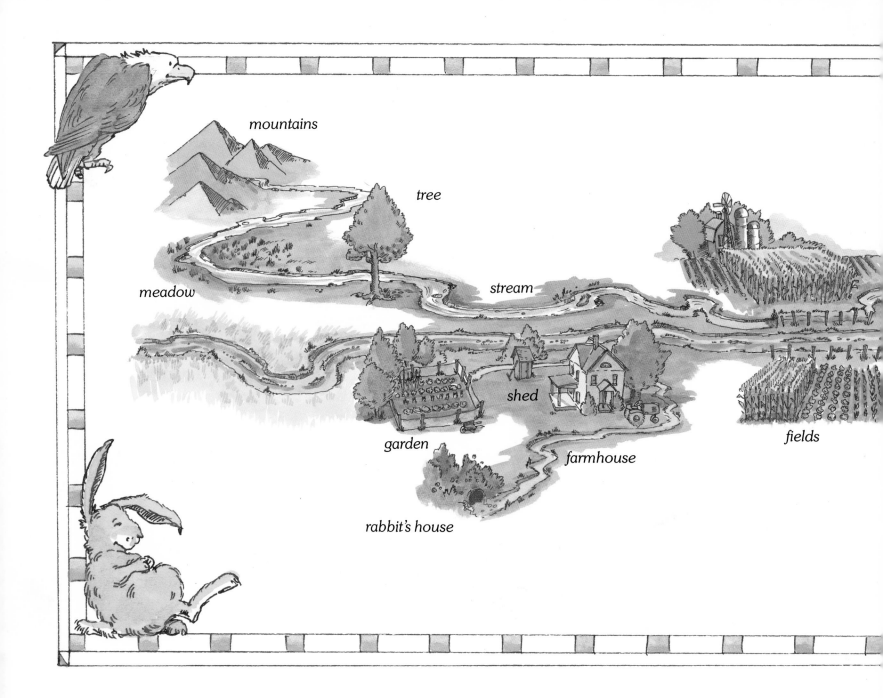

mountains

tree

meadow

stream

shed

garden

farmhouse

fields

rabbit's house

30

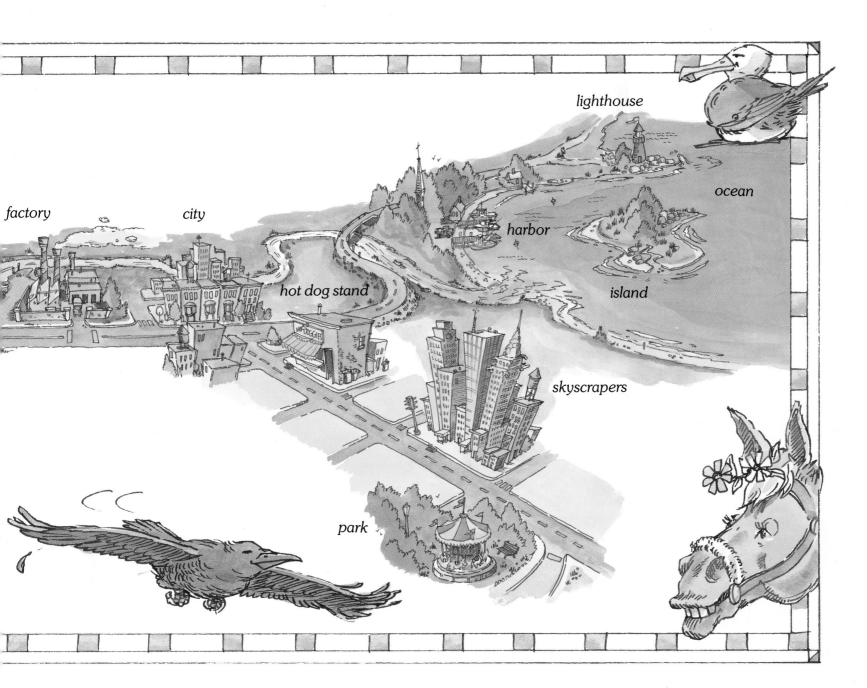

factory

city

lighthouse

ocean

harbor

hot dog stand

island

skyscrapers

park

THE BIG MAP